fresco

SEA OF CRETE

CRETE

Knossos •

• Mallia

Mt. Dicte

• Phaistos

MEDITERRANEAN SEA

The ancient civilisation which today we call Minoan Crete was one of great splendour and technical achievement comparable in some cases with that of the twentieth century. Scholars still debate its many aspects, and archaeologists continue to search for further clues to widen our knowledge of the Minoans.

Here is the story of Crete as we believe it was in those far-off days, with its gay people and rich life.

CONTENTS

The story of the Minotaur

There were once three king's sons who lived in Crete. One of these was called Minos. When his father died, Minos said that he should be king because the gods would do whatever he told them to do. To prove this he set up an altar on the sea-shore. There he prayed to Poseidon, god of the sea, to send him a bull, which he promised to sacrifice back to the god. No sooner had Minos spoken than a splendid white bull came out of the sea. All the people watching saw that the gods did as Minos commanded and they made him their king.

But Minos did not keep his promise to Poseidon. He was so pleased with the white bull that he kept it and sacrificed another. The god of the sea was angry with Minos and punished him. He made Minos' wife fall in love with the bull. She had a child which grew up with the body of a man but the head of a bull.

His mother called him 'Asterion' but everyone else called him the 'Minotaur' – or 'the bull of Minos'. Not only did the Minotaur have the head of a bull, he also had its nature. He was a savage animal, not a person.

King Minos felt that he had to have him shut away, so he ordered a labyrinth to be built. This was a great dark maze, full of winding passages. Here in the darkness the terrible monster was kept.

Theseus kills the Minotaur

Minos was a cruel king. When the people of Athens killed his son, he ordered them to send to Crete seven youths and seven maidens. This they had to do every year. When the Athenian youths and girls arrived in Crete, King Minos fed them to the Minotaur.

Because the Athenians were so afraid of King Minos, they sent off the youths and maidens two years in succession. When the king sent a third request, the Athenians sadly made preparations to send off the victims. This time, however, the son of the king of Athens, Theseus, was there. He was already a great hero, and he said he would go as one of the victims and try to kill the Minotaur.

Theseus was lucky. Because he was so handsome, Minos' daughter Ariadne fell in love with him. She said she would help Theseus kill the Minotaur if he would marry her. Theseus, of course, said he would.

Ariadne then led Theseus to the great door of the labyrinth where she gave him a magic ball of string. This ball of string had been given to her by Daedalus, the man who had built the labyrinth. When one end of the string was tied to the door-post, the ball would unwind itself into the darkness and roll all the way to the Minotaur. Theseus quickly tied the string to the door-post and followed the ball of string into the darkness. When he came to the middle of the labyrinth, he found the monster asleep. After killing him, he followed the string back to the entrance where Ariadne and the other Athenians were waiting for him.

They all jumped quickly into a waiting ship and sailed away from Crete.

Daedalus the magic craftsman

Daedalus was the man who built the labyrinth for Minos. He was a most amazing person. There was nothing he could not do and no problem he could not solve. He was an inventor, scientist, architect, magician, all rolled into one.

He had come from Athens and had been made welcome in Crete by Minos. After a time Daedalus grew tired of living in Crete, but because he was so valuable, Minos would not let him leave. This only set Daedalus another problem. King Minos controlled the land and sea but he did not control the air. Daedalus got to work. He collected feathers and wax from which he made two pairs of wings. One pair was for himself, the other for his young son Icarus.

Before they flew away, Daedalus warned his son not to fly too high or the wax would melt. Then he took off, followed by Icarus. They flew over the sea and for a time all was well. But then Icarus became too confident and flew higher and higher, nearer the sun. The wax on his wings melted, the feathers fell from his arms and down he plunged into the sea and drowned.

After burying his son in Italy, Daedalus flew on to Sicily where he stayed with King Cocalus. Minos however found out where he was and came to fetch him back. The daughters of King Cocalus did not want Daedalus to leave because he had made them some magic dolls that could walk, and so they arranged for King Minos to be killed.

After Minos' death, Crete was never as powerful again.

Memories and poems

The Greeks who lived in Classical times, i.e. between 500 B C and 400 B C, believed that long ago there had been a real king of Crete called Minos. He was a wealthy but cruel ruler of a mighty empire, which he controlled with a powerful fleet of ships. Minos also had lived in a great palace, surrounded by monsters and magicians. The Greeks thought that after they themselves died they would meet Minos again, because he had become a great judge in the world of Death, under the ground.

It is important to notice that these Greeks got their knowledge about Crete from myths, legends and stories. There were no history books on Crete written by Minos or Daedalus. There were no palaces left standing for them to see. All the evidence for the civilisation of Crete came from tradition. We are so used to reading words which are printed that we find this hard to understand. In ancient civilisations writing and reading played a much smaller part than it does today.

The stories about Minos and Daedalus were remembered and handed down by word of mouth. The easiest way to remember something is to make a poem about it and sing it. This is the way many of the legends, often thousands of lines long, were preserved. To be able to compose and remember long poems was a special skill. In the courts of the kings there were poets who could do just this. The picture opposite shows one such poet, the bard Phemius, singing a poem.

The *Iliad* of Homer is an example of a poem which tells a story. It tells of the fighting over the city of Troy, which was supposedly destroyed in 1184 B C. The *Iliad* was not written down until much later. For hundreds of years the poem had been remembered and passed down by word of mouth.

Passing information on by word of mouth over the centuries is a very hit and miss business however, and we need something else, other than the myths and legends about Crete. This is where archaeology helps.

Sir Arthur Evans

We believe today that the myths and legends do tell us something about the Greeks. A hundred years ago most people thought that there was no truth at all behind the great stories like the *Iliad* and *Odyssey*. One person took a different view. He was a German called Heinrich Schliemann. When he read in the *Iliad* about a city called Troy, he thought that there must have been such a city. He felt that if he looked carefully enough, he would find what was left of it. Many people thought he was foolish. Schliemann astounded the world, however, when he discovered the site of the city of Troy, where the stories said Helen and Paris had lived. Schliemann's discoveries made other people become interested in archaeology.

One such person was Arthur Evans. He was a rich Englishman whose first clue to an ancient Cretan civilisation came from seal-stones engraved with hieroglyphics or small pictures. Modern peasant women had picked them out of the soil to wear as 'charms' to ward off ill-luck. One is illustrated on page 19.

It was Arthur Evans who excavated the palace at Knossos. It took him over thirty years to do this. Not only did he excavate the site of the palace but he also spent his fortune on rebuilding and restoring parts of it. In this he was helped by a team of archaeologists, artists and builders. Some modern archaeologists do not agree with the way he excavated the palace and the way he restored it, but no one can deny that he was the person who discovered there was an ancient civilisation on Crete. He called this civilisation *Minoan* after King Minos. This is why we talk today about the Minoans.

The discoveries of the archaeologists

Archaeologists have discovered many things about the civilisation of Crete which we could not find in the myths and legends. We now know that the first people to inhabit Crete were hunters and fishermen who crossed over to the island about 6000 B C, probably from what is now Turkey. They were a Stone Age people and at first lived in caves. Later they became farmers as well as hunters and fishermen. They also learned to build houses with mud walls.

Although we do not know many details, it seems that life became more civilised about 2600 B C. The discovery of bronze changed the lives of the Stone Age people and gave them a different world. There is a further change about 2000 B C. Many important developments must have taken place from 3000 B C to 2600 B C.

In about 1900 B C the first palaces were built in Crete, at Knossos, Phaistos and Mallia. These palaces were destroyed in about 1700 B C, probably by an earthquake. New and bigger palaces were then built on the ruins of the old ones. Archaeologists call the period from 2000 B C to 1700 B C the 'First Palace Period', and the period from 1700 B C to 1400 B C the 'Second Palace Period'. In about 1450 B C the palaces were again destroyed, again perhaps by an earthquake. This time they were not rebuilt. The Cretan civilisation was at its height during the Second Palace Period. After 1450 B C Crete was no longer powerful.

THE EARLY HISTORY OF CRETE

5000 B C - 2600 B C. Neolithic or New Stone Age in Crete. *First known inhabitants: hunters, fishermen, farmers.*

2600 B C - 2000 B C. Pre-Palace Period. *Quiet progress.*

2000 B C - 1700 B C. First Palace Period. *First palaces built.*

1700 B C - 1400 B C. Second Palace Period. *Palaces rebuilt. Minoans at their greatest.*

1400 B C - 1150 B C. Post-Palace Period. *Minoans no longer powerful.*

Problems with archaeology

We now know much more about the Minoan civilisation because of what the archaeologists have discovered, but even archaeologists cannot tell us everything we would like to know. Archaeologists look for evidence in the same way that detectives look for clues. They search for bits and pieces of things out of which they can build up a true picture of a civilisation. It is very hard to get a true picture of Cretan civilisation, for much of the evidence has been destroyed completely.

Secondly what has been found is only one kind of evidence. We have found palaces, pottery, jewellery, and wall paintings, but we have *not* found Minoan ships, soldiers' uniforms, patterns for dresses, nor accounts of what Minoan women cooked. We don't know how the king governed, how many slaves there were, nor the names of ordinary people.

Even the clues which we have are sometimes hard to understand. Although we can get some idea of what Minoan women wore from the paintings on the walls of the palaces, these paintings only tell us about *some* women. They were probably princesses or ladies of the court. We have no idea what other women would wear.

On the opposite page you can see some of the evidence which archaeologists have found. 1. and 7. are *rhytons* or drinking vessels ; 2. is a pendant showing a god of nature ; 3. is a seal showing a priest holding a sacred bird; 4. is a queen's necklace from a royal tomb in central Crete ; 5. is a Minoan cup from Phaistos; and 6. is a hieroglyphic seal.

1

2

3

4

5

6

7

The palace at Knossos

The most famous Cretan palace was found at Knossos. It was built about 1700 B C. This palace was huge; it covered several acres and had 1,300 rooms. Although we do not know what many of these rooms were used for, we have at least some idea of what went on in some important areas of the palace. On the plan of the palace at the end of the book, you will notice the following five areas.

1   The Central Courtyard. This was an open yard, paved with slabs of limestone. The courtyard was 60 yards (54·8 m) long and over 30 yards (27·4 m) wide, and may have been used for religious ceremonies.

2   On the west side of the courtyard were the official rooms of the palace. This is where the king would conduct state business; here he would welcome ambassadors from Egypt or Greece. Here too he might have been worshipped. In this area of the palace is the Throne Room, illustrated on page 29.

3   Beyond the official part of the palace were the store-rooms. These contained the huge pithoi – clay jars sometimes as tall as men – for storing olive oil, corn and wine. 150 pithoi were found in the store-rooms, but there was room for about 400. This would mean that the king could store over 1,700 gallons (7728 litres) of oil in this part of the palace if he wanted to.

4   On the south east side of the Central Court were the private rooms of the king. Among these was a set of rooms which must have belonged to the queen. These rooms were beautifully decorated and had a private bath and a flushing lavatory.

5   To the north of the king's rooms were many work-shops. Here different sorts of craftsmen – stone-masons, potters, goldsmiths, silversmiths, and jewellers – worked for the king.

The palace had four entrances, marked on the plan as A, B, C, and D. Visitors who came to see the king on official business would enter the palace by A – the western entrance.

The building of the palace

It was not easy to build a palace that had 1,300 rooms and four or five floors. To start with, the site where the palace was to be built had to be carefully prepared. The builders had to bring together, from Crete and elsewhere, all the materials they needed. Stone had to be cut from quarries in the mountains and brought to the site along rough roads. This was a slow business and very expensive. When the stone arrived at a site, it had to be cut by the masons to the right shape and size.

Different sorts of stone were used for different parts of the palace, according to whether protection was needed from the weather or a decorative finish was required. They used alabaster (a kind of marble) to face the floors and the walls, particularly in the great halls and bathrooms. The alabaster was cut very carefully into large sheets only 1 inch (25 mm) thick. In other parts of the palace the builders used a lot of limestone.

Cypress trees were also cut from the forests, trimmed, and transported to the site. Here they would be made into beams for the roofs and ceilings, floorboards for the upper stories, window frames and doors, and many other things.

The builders of the palace used clay, too. Just like the stone and the wood, the clay had to be dug out, brought to the site, and prepared for use. In building the palace they put the clay to many different uses. They mixed it with straw or seaweed to make bricks for the palace walls. They used it to fill in walls, and also to cover flat roofs to protect them from the weather.

Furnishing the palace at Knossos

Besides builders, masons and carpenters, many other people helped to build the palace at Knossos. Painters, sculptors, and metal workers were all employed to make the palace beautiful. Others, too, would have been very busy furnishing the palace. It must have needed great quantities of chairs, tables, serving dishes, plates and drinking vessels, lamps and curtains in its 1,300 rooms. No doubt the craftsmen who made the things would spend a long time working on them until they were perfect. Kings are known to be very fussy, they want the best. It takes time to make something for a king.

We do not know how long it took to build the palace at Knossos. Certainly it would have been finished in a shorter time than it took to build our mediaeval cathedrals which, in some cases, took over a hundred years. One thing is interesting about the way the palace was built. Nearly everything was made on the site. We can imagine a whole series of builders' yards springing up near the site of the palace. In them would be made all the window frames, paving slabs, and pillars that were to be parts of the palace.

The palace at Knossos was built about 1700 B C. We know that the Minoans had built other palaces before. Even so perhaps the most remarkable thing about this palace is the skill of the architect who built it. He took great care over small details. For example, at the eastern entrance rain water was skilfully channelled down the steps, and disappeared as if by magic. The Greek for skilful or magical is *diadalos*. If there ever was a real king of Crete called Minos, a real architect called Daedalus may well have built the palace for him.

The atmosphere of the palace

The palace at Knossos was the most amazing building in the world of its day. This was not only because it was so large and had parts which were four or five stories high. It was also remarkable for the thousands of different things it contained. It was more like a city than a house.

If you walked through it, you would find staircases and corridors, passages and colonnades. Some parts were open to the sun and rain, other parts were covered over. Some places – for example where treasure was kept – were sealed up. Some areas of the palace were very plain, others covered with wall paintings. The wall paintings show many different aspects of Minoan life. You can see very smart young Minoan ladies, wearing lipstick and with elegant hair styles, brave young men and girls jumping over a bull's back, and pictures of shields made of cowhide.

If you looked at some of the different objects the palace contained, you might notice the huge storage jars, some of which were bigger than a man, or the tiny moulds used for making gold earrings in the shape of a bull's horns, or a gaming board made of gold, silver and lapis lazuli (a dark blue semi-precious stone).

You might, too, notice the shape of a double axe which was carved on a wall by one of the stone masons. The Greek word for a double axe is *labrys*, and the word *labyrinth* means the house of the double axe. Labyrinth also came to mean the house of fear. If you were a young Athenian about to go to Crete, you might well believe the palace was the labyrinth, and Minos not the king, but the terrible Minotaur.

The owner of the palace

We do not know who owned the palace, but we can tell something about him from the palace itself. The palace at Knossos was built *for* a king and *by* a king. Just like Buckingham Palace, it was meant to be the home for a royal family. Here the king would live with his wife and children. Like Buckingham Palace, it was also a state house, where the king welcomed other kings and princes to stay. It was also the seat of government where the king met his ministers and where, too, all the official records were kept. In this respect the palace was like the House of Commons and Whitehall; it contained the government and civil service. The palace was also a great business centre, making things to use and sell.

We can build up a picture of the owner, who was a king, very wealthy, living in his huge palace with his family and guests, governing a mighty empire with the help of his ministers and at the same time running a series of businesses. The remains of the palace, however, show that the owner was more than this. He was also the head of the Cretan religion. He seems to have been worshipped as a god by the Minoans.

A fine wall painting in the palace shows a young handsome Minoan prince leading an animal to sacrifice. The prince is bare to the waist; on his head he wears a crown of lilies, out of which stands the long tail of a peacock. Sir Arthur Evans thought that this was a picture of the young ruler, who was not only a king; he was a priest and a god as well.

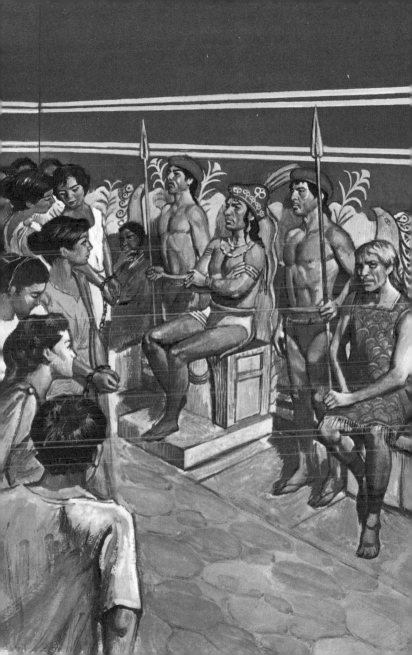

Private houses

Not all Minoans lived in the great palaces. Many lived in towns, villages and farms throughout Crete. We do not know very clearly what their houses were like but we do have one piece of evidence which shows us what some of the Minoan houses were like. In the remains of the palace at Knossos mosaic panels were found which show some town houses.

Each house in the mosaic is only between 30-50 mm high but they are meant to represent real houses. From these we can see that the houses the Minoans built for themselves in towns were tall, towerlike buildings. Most of them had flat roofs, on top of which were built square shaped attics. The houses were of different designs. Some were built two stories high, others three or four. Some were quite small, having only a single door and two windows. Others were larger than this.

The pieces of the mosaic show that some houses had as many as six windows in the front; the frames of the windows are made of wood and the windows are covered over, probably with skins or matting. There is not a single house which has a window on the ground floor. This suggests that the owners lived in the rooms upstairs and kept the ground floor free for other purposes.

The walls of the houses were built of stone cemented together in layers with clay.

Farming

Farming in ancient Crete was just as varied as it is today, and many Minoans worked on the land. On the right you can see a picture based on a harvest scene which a Minoan artist carved on a stone vase. Here we see some farm workers coming home after a day's work in the fields. They have been busy in the olive groves. The men march along the road in twos, carrying long poles on top of which are sharp hooks. They have been using these poles to knock down the olives off the trees. One man carries a *sistrum* – a sort of rattle – and is singing for all he is worth. The man leading wears a quilted jerkin.

When the olives were brought to the farms, they were put into vats of hot water and crushed. The oil came out of the olives and floated on top of the water, which was then drained off.

The Minoans also grew corn and grapes. They reared cattle and kept bees. They hunted in the woods for wild goats and birds. They fished the seas for octopus, and shell fish such as the *murex* or sea-mussel, which gave purple dye.

They were also skilful shepherds. In the eastern part of the island a bowl has been found which is decorated on the inside with the figures of a shepherd and his flock. The shepherd is sitting at the back of his flock of over 200 sheep, who graze contentedly on the side of the hill. The sheep would provide the Minoans with meat and wool, amongst other things.

Bronze, gold and stone

The Minoans were skilful craftsmen, particularly with bronze and gold. Before iron and steel were invented, bronze (a mixture of copper and tin) was the most commonly used metal. The Minoans used bronze to make all sorts of weapons: swords, daggers, axes; and all sorts of tools from tweezers to crowbars. They also made large cauldrons out of bronze. Some of these have been found. One of the biggest of them is nearly 4 feet (1·2 m) in diameter and weighs almost 115 lb (52·2 kg). It is made out of seven separate sheets of bronze, all held together by rivets. The Minoans thought very highly of bronze. They even made some of their clay vessels in the shape of metal ones and put on them imitation clay rivets.

The Minoans were also very good at working with stone. They made many different shapes of vases from stone, on some of which they carved pictures. Archaeologists have also found many seals made of precious stones, such as brown agate, red and green jasper, and rock crystal. One seal has two horses carved on it, another has two fish, and a third a wild goat. The seals were used to stamp an owner's mark on clay.

The Minoans were excellent goldsmiths. Many small objects have been found which are made of gold. One of the best is the gold pendant shown opposite, which was made before 1600 B C. The pendant shows two queen bees facing each other, sideways on. In their legs they hold a heavy honeycomb. They are both sucking at a round drop of honey. From this pendant we can learn how skilled the Minoan craftsmen were. We know they could make thin leaves of gold: on this pendant the gold leaf was used for the bees' wings. They could make gold wire: here it was used for the bees' legs. They could solder gold to gold: here they joined the two bees by their heads and abdomens. They could also make small granules of gold, one by one, and fix them together to make the honeycomb or to decorate the bees' bodies.

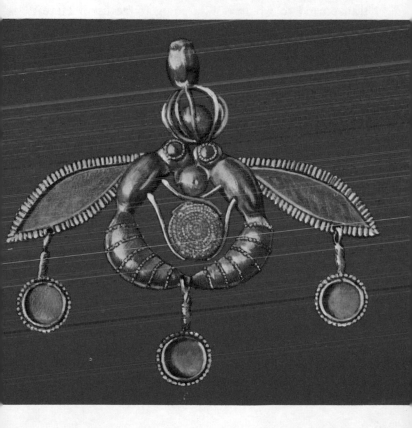

Pottery

It is difficult for us to imagine a world in which there was nothing made of paper, nothing made of plastic and very few things made of metal. Such raw materials as there were in ancient Crete were used in many different ways. A good example of this is the way in which the Minoans used clay.

Making things out of clay was a great industry in Crete. The clay had to be dug out of the ground and transported to where it was going to be used. Here it had to be prepared for the potter and the kiln. This meant that the clay had to be *wedged up*. This means it had to have all the air beaten out of it so that it did not explode when it was fired in the kiln. When the clay was wedged up, it was ready for the potter to use either with his hands alone or on the wheel. The picture opposite shows some of the activities that went on in a pottery.

Minoan potters made many things out of clay: things for the house, such as cups, jugs and vases; things for trade, such as the giant storage jars; and things to offer the gods, such as little figures of animals or dancing women.

Some of these objects have been skilfully decorated with designs from the sea – octopus, shell fish, starfish, seaweed; or from nature – papyrus reeds, palm trees, or flowers. Other pots have snakes on them, or double axes; some are decorated with lines, spirals, curves and shapes. Sometimes the decoration is made within the clay. At other times the potter put on different glazes, which when fired in the kiln produced patterns of different colours. A glaze is what potters use as a form of paint.

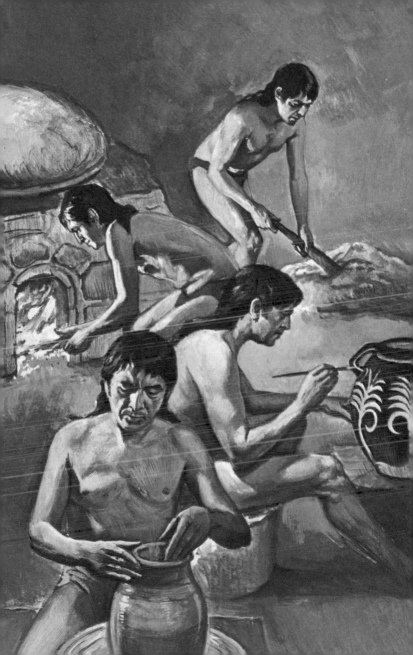

Trade

One of the mysteries about the Minoans is the fact that their towns and palaces did not have any great walls or fortifications round them. Some people think that the Minoans did not need walls to protect them because they had such a powerful navy. With this powerful navy they built up and controlled a great empire.

What we do know is that the Minoans were great traders. Everything that went in or out of Crete had to come by sea. We can imagine that they would have different sorts of ships. Large ones that sailed the seas, with high prows and low sterns and square sails set on a central mast. There would also be small boats working only in the harbours, loading and unloading the bigger boats. They may also have had fighting ships to attack their enemies or defend their empire.

The Minoans exported wines, olive oil, wood and textiles. They also sold abroad things which they themselves had made. Two gold cups which were made in Crete have been found at Vapheio in Greece. At Mycene two splendid daggers from Crete have been found too. To make such objects the Minoans had to import things which Crete did not have. They brought from Egypt ivory which they made into little figures of men and animals. From Egypt, too, came precious stones to turn into seals, *faience* (glazed pottery) for decorating gaming boards and chairs, and ostrich eggs. Copper and tin were imported from Asia Minor to turn into lamps, jugs, cauldrons and pots.

The Minoans do not seem to have used coins or money. Where they had to pay for things, they seem to have used a system of exchange or barter.

The women

The wall paintings which were found at Knossos show us how some of the Minoan women dressed. They wore long skirts and blouses. The skirts were either plain or flounced. The blouses had short puffed sleeves and were open fronted to show off their breasts. Their hair was carefully arranged and was twisted round with strings of beads and jewels. Some women wore hair bands, others had turban-like head-dresses.

Minoan women seem to have had an important part in public life. This is rare in ancient civilisations. In some ways they seem to have been more important than the men. They took part in the bull leaping games. They were also priestesses and took the major part in some religious ceremonies. They sat in the best seats at the front, whenever shows were put on. It is interesting to notice, too, that on the wall paintings in the palace at Knossos, the women are painted in more detail than the men.

The Minoan women also took part in the religious dances that were put on in the great courtyards of the palaces. They had dances called 'The Labyrinth', 'Daedalus', and 'The Bulls'. We find the best description of such a dance in the *Iliad* of Homer. Here is a translation of it.

"The God Hephaistos made a shield for the Greek hero Achilles. On part of this shield he made an image of a dancing floor, just like the one which Daedalus once designed in the broad palace of Knossos for the lovely-haired Ariadne. On the dancing floor danced young men and pretty young girls, in lines, each holding the other by the wrists. Here they ran round lightly on their nimble feet moving as smoothly as a potter's wheel in the hands of a skilled potter. There they ran in lines to meet each other. This fine dance attracted a great crowd, who enjoyed themselves watching. In the middle of them a god-like bard sang and played on his lyre, while two acrobats turned somersaults in and out of the crowd in time to the music."

Bulls

The animal which is most commonly connected with Crete is the bull. The Greeks believed that Zeus turned himself into a bull and carried the young girl Europa off to Crete. In Greek legend, Europa is the mother of King Minos. The Minotaur legend itself may have arisen through the Minoans' fear of earthquakes, which they could not understand. The rumblings which could be heard from time to time might well have been taken for the roaring of a great bull beneath the ground. The bull was certainly very important to the Minoans, for in the caves around the island archaeologists have found little figures of bulls put there as offerings to the gods. In the palaces, too, vessels have been found, made of precious stones and metals, in the shape of bulls' heads. Parts of the same palaces are decorated with bulls' horns, carved in stone.

The most famous piece of evidence is the wall painting found in a small courtyard in the east wing of the palace at Knossos. The wall painting shows three acrobats leaping over the back of a huge bull. The acrobat had to attract the bull's attention and get it to charge. When the bull charged, the acrobat caught hold of the bull's horns in both hands. Then, as the bull tossed its head, the acrobat had to somersault over it and land on its back. Young girls as well as men played this dangerous game. To start with they were often princes and princesses, but later on, slaves were trained to entertain in this way.

To be a good bull leaper, you would need to be swift on your feet, have a keen eye, strong arms and a good sense of balance. You would also need partners to help you. Bull leaping must have been a team effort.

Writing

In ancient civilisations writing and reading played a much smaller part than they do today. In Minoan times there were no newspapers, no printing presses, no books, no paper. Archaeologists have found three separate forms of writing in Crete.

Picture writing or hieroglyphics This appeared on Crete about 2000 B C, and was used until 1650 B C. This writing is found on the seals made of stone and their clay impressions. It consists of little pictures (pictograms) of objects, for example, a ship, fish, bird, man, hand, axe, and a jug.

Linear A This was the form of writing that appeared later than the picture writing. It was made up of lines, either straight or curved. This started to appear on Crete about 1700 B C. Although this was the writing in use at the time of the building of the great palaces at Knossos and elsewhere, no one has worked out what it means.

Linear B Another form of line writing has been found which appeared in about 1450 B C. This has been called Linear B. It uses the same lines as Linear A, but at first was thought to be quite a different language. It has been found on clay tablets at Knossos in Crete and at Mycene, Pylos and Thebes on mainland Greece. The Linear B tablets seem to be records of what the palace had in stock.

They do raise a problem. What was the connection between Crete and Greece? Did the Cretans rule the Greeks or the Greeks the Cretans? The person who deciphered Linear B suggested that the Minoans were Greeks, since Linear B appeared to be a very old kind of Greek.

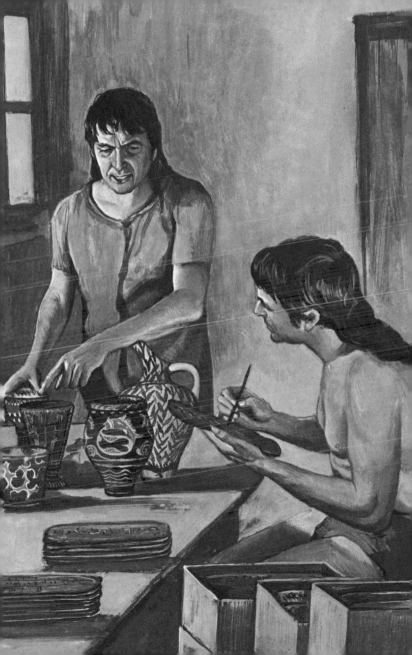

Minoan worship

We know that the inhabitants of the island of Crete were religious. Archaeologists have found altars, shrines, sacred caves, statues, temples and many other things which show that they did worship something. We know too, from the small statues which have been found, that when they prayed the men held their left arm by their side and shielded their eyes with their right hand. The women prayed standing erect with their hands underneath their breasts.

In Minoan times the most important object of worship was not a god but a goddess. The Minoans worshipped a mother goddess, who can be seen in the picture opposite. Although we do not know her name she appears in many different forms. Sometimes she appears as an animal, and she is often seen as a snake.

We can get some idea of what sort of goddess she was from the story that the Greeks told about their goddess, Demeter, centuries later. Demeter means in Greek 'Mother Earth'. She had a daughter who was stolen by the King of Death and taken under the ground. After a long search Demeter found her child, but could only get the King of Death to allow her to come back to earth for six months of every year. Demeter's daughter is the corn seed which, after lying in the ground for so long, grows and ripens on the earth in the spring and summer months. In worshipping Demeter, the Greeks were doing three things. They were giving honour to a powerful goddess, they were honouring Nature, and they were connecting their own happiness with religion and Nature. The Minoans may have felt something like this for their own mother goddess.

Cretan-born Zeus

While the main object of worship in Minoan times was the mother goddess, the Minoans also worshipped a god. This god is sometimes seen as the mother goddess's son; at other times he is her husband. Sometimes he is both her son and husband. The mother goddess is ageless, but the god is a young man.

In Minoan times the mother goddess was the more important of the two. In Mycenean times (i.e. after 1400 B C), the young god became more important. It is he who turns into Zeus, the great king of the gods worshipped by the Greeks in later times. There are many legends that connect Zeus with Crete.

Many Greeks of Classical times believed that Zeus had been born in a cave on Mount Dicte, a mountain in Crete. This is where Zeus's mother, Rhea, had fled to by night to save her child from being swallowed by Cronos, his father. Cronos had been told that one of his children would overthrow him and be king of the world in his place. To prevent this, he used to swallow his children as they were born. When Zeus was born, Rhea hid him away on Mount Dicte, and tricked Cronos into swallowing a stone instead. Zeus grew up and waged war on Cronos, defeating him.

The inhabitants of Crete in later times used to say that Zeus was born again every year in his cave in Crete, with a flashing fire and a great stream of blood. They believed that he died every year, was buried and rose from the grave.

Archaeologists have found many different kinds of offerings to the gods in the cave on Mount Dicte, both from Classical times and Minoan times.

Destruction and decay

No one is quite sure how the Minoan civilisation came to an end. We do know that the very first palaces that had been built on Crete were destroyed about 1700 B C, probably by an earthquake. But this destruction gave the Minoans the opportunity to build bigger and better palaces. The great time for building was after 1700 B C and this time is the high point of the Minoan civilisation. Round about 1450 B C the palaces were again destroyed.

No one knows exactly why this happened. Some people believe that the palaces were destroyed by invaders from Greece. We have already seen that there were connections between Crete and Mycene – the daggers and Linear B tablets. We also know that the Lion Gateway in Mycene was built under Minoan influence. It is true, too, that after 1450 B C the city of Mycene became the head of a great new empire. If we add all this evidence up, it could have been the Myceneans who destroyed the palaces and took over what had been Minos' empire.

Other archaeologists have offered different explanations. There is an island called Santorin which lies 100 miles (160·9 km) to the north of Crete. We know that in about 1450 B C there was a volcanic eruption which tore the island apart. A great wave of water swept over parts of Crete, which was also showered with volcanic ash. This violent eruption was preceded by a series of earthquakes. Some people believe that it was this that destroyed the palaces.

What is clear is that after 1450 B C neither Crete nor the Minoans were ever so powerful again. It was with Mycene and the kings there that the future lay.

INDEX